D0548858

this ·little·barron's· book belongs to

....

....

First edition for the United States and Canada published 1999 by
Barron's Educational Series, Inc.

Copyright © Nicola Smee 1999

First published in Great Britain by Orchard Books in 1999.

All inquiries should be addressed to:
Barron's Educational Series, Inc.
250 Wireless Boulevard, Hauppauge, New York 11788
http://www.barronseduc.com

Library of Congress Catalog Card No.: 98-74974
International Standard Book No. 0-7641-0873-5

Printed in Italy

9 8 7 6 5 4 3 2 1

Freddie Gets a Haircut

Nicola Smee

• l i t t l e • b a r r o n ' s •

"It's time for a haircut, Freddie!"
says Mom.

Bear wants to come
and watch.

"Hello, Freddie! Hello, Bear!"
says Bob, the hairdresser.

Hello,
Bob!

I tell him to be careful not to snip my ears!

"Here, pick a lollipop, Freddie, and take one home for Bear," says Bob.

Freddie,
you look LOVELY!